THE CASE OF THE
SNOWBOUND SPY

By the Same Author

The Case of the Snowbound Spy

A McGURK MYSTERY

BY E. W. HILDICK
ILLUSTRATED BY LISL WEIL

MACMILLAN PUBLISHING CO., INC.
New York

Macmillan Publishing Co., Inc.
866 Third Avenue, New York, N.Y. 10022
Collier Macmillan Canada, Ltd.

Printed in the United States of America

10 9 8 7 6 5 4 3 2 1

Library of Congress Cataloging in Publication Data
Hildick, Edmund Wallace.   The case of the snowbound spy.
(A McGurk mystery)
Summary: The McGurk sleuths accept a job from a stranger in town,
only to find they are assisting in high-level industrial espionage.
[1. Mystery and detective stories] I. Weil, Lisl. II. Title.
PZ7.H5463Carc   [Fic]   80-12272   ISBN 0-02-743860-0

For A3, A14, A17, A8, and A18

Contents

THE CASE OF THE SNOWBOUND SPY

1 The Strange Letter

This case started on a Saturday morning. It had been snowing all through Friday night—the second fairly heavy snowfall of the winter. It had dumped another six or seven inches on the snow that had fallen only a few days before.

Naturally, that meant most of us kids were busy shoveling the stuff off our driveways. So who can blame me for answering McGurk with one word when he called?

"No!" I said, as I picked up the phone.

"'No'?" came his yelp. "What d'you mean—'No'? I haven't asked you anything yet!"

He sounded hurt as well as sore. I could almost

see the freckles bunch up around his green eyes.

"I know you haven't," I said. "But I don't have to be a detective to guess what's coming, Jack P. McGurk!"

"Oh, yeah?"

"Yeah," I said. "You're going to suggest one of your Saturday morning specials. A special training session for the McGurk Organization. Right?"

"I—"

"You're going to say why don't we all stop by at your place and help shovel *your* driveway."

"But—"

"You're going to say you've buried some stuff there in the snow. So we can see who turns up the most. Training to find clues in deep snow. Right?"

"*Wrong!* I—"

"You bet it's wrong, McGurk. Because nothing doing. I'm busy on *my* driveway. You do your own shoveling!"

There was the sound of a deep breath. Then his voice came through loud and clear.

"For your information, Joey Rockaway, my dad—uh—and me—we finished clearing our driveway an hour ago. This"—(his voice took on a jeering note)—"is to tell you we've got a case."

There was nothing phony about that ring of triumph.

"Oh?" I said.

"Yeah. A letter. It arrived just a few minutes ago. Whoever sent it is offering five dollars a day plus expenses."

"For what? What kind of case?"

Some of the confidence left his voice then.

"Well, it doesn't exactly say, but—"

"And what do you mean—'whoever sent it'?" I said, suspicious again.

"It doesn't say that, either. Just about the fee and expenses. The rest—the rest of it's in code."

"In *code*?"

All at once my interest had returned.

"Yeah. I guess it's a test. To see how smart we are."

"Well, I'm pretty good at codes," I said.

"That's what I'm counting on, Officer Rockaway," said McGurk, sounding very official and a bit grim. "This one's a real toughie, believe me. So hurry. Finish your shoveling and get over here. I'll call the others. Who knows? Brains might beat you to it. Or Wanda. Or even Willie. And I mean beat you to *cracking the code!*"

That was enough for me.

I finished clearing the driveway in ten minutes flat.

2 The Code

McGurk must have taken less time than that to do his whole shoveling job—with or without the help of his father. Their driveway was a mess—with big chunks of hard-packed snow still studding it. Three times I nearly slipped, hurrying along there. And the path around the back, leading to the basement steps, hadn't been cleared at all. Just stomped down by several pairs of feet.

The others *had* beaten me to it getting there.

Brains Bellingham, Wanda Grieg and Willie Sandowsky were standing in front of the big table. Pools of melting snow were spreading at their feet. But that didn't worry McGurk, sitting there in his

rocking chair at the head of the table. His red hair was tousled from heavy scratching and his eyes gleamed with eagerness and impatience.

"O.K., *Code Expert*!" he said. "Shut the door and take a look at *this*."

"This" was the sheet of paper lying on the table. The others were staring at it like they were hypnotized. Next to it was an envelope, neatly typed, addressed to "The McGurk Organization." Also neatly typed was the message itself. Or at least the

first part of the message. The rest—well . . . . Here it
is: the whole thing. See what *you* make of it.

URGENTLY NEED YOUR HELP ON

AN IMPORTANT ASSIGNMENT.

WILL PAY FIVE DOLLARS A

DAY PLUS EXPENSES.

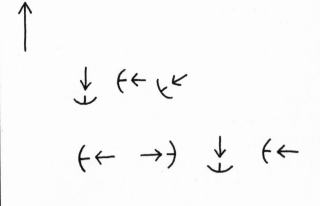

Like that.

Block capital letters, with a grease spot on the side.

Then the crazy signs—done by hand, probably with a ballpoint pen.

"Hm!" I said, reaching to pick it up.

"Use these!" snapped Brains, rapping my knuckles with a pair of tweezers.

He sounded mad. His short hair seemed to bristle even more than usual. His eyes flashed behind his big glasses. I guess he was miffed at not solving the code before I got there—him being our science expert and all.

"There's no need to pick it up anyway," said Wanda, breaking off nibbling her lip and tossing back a wing of her long blond hair. She's our climbing expert—but I guess when it comes to codes everyone wants to get into the act. "There's nothing on the other side. Right, McGurk?"

McGurk nodded.

"And Willie can't even get a whiff of anything from that grease spot. So it's up to you, Officer Rockaway."

Willie Sandowsky looked sad. He fingered his long thin nose. He's our sniffing expert: "owner of the most sensitive nose in the business," according to McGurk.

"I got another cold," mumbled Willie. "And when I got a cold, my nose is just like anyone else's."

"Yeah—smellwise!" snapped Brains. "But in size and shape—"

"Be quiet!" said McGurk. (They really *were* getting mad over what I *thought* was maybe a very simple code. Hmm . . . .) "Be quiet and let the expert take a good look."

"Yes," said Wanda, pushing Brains to one side. "I —"

"Not *you!*" growled McGurk. "All *you* could think of was that it looked like stitches from a needlework pattern. *Stitches!*"

"Well it does *so!* That might be the base for the code. And they're more like stitches than snowflakes, anyway," Wanda added, glaring at Brains.

Brains glared back.

"I said snow *crystals*. Far more scientific than snow*flakes*."

"I still think shorthand," said Willie. "My mom used to be a secretary. She has this book—"

"So stop yacking about it and go get it!" said McGurk. "You just may be right."

Willie went. Brains sniffed.

"He's wasting his time," he said. "I know a bit about shorthand. And *this*"—he waved at the signs— "comes from no shorthand system *I* ever heard of. Not Pitman, not Gregg . . . ."

I let them all ramble on. It was giving me more time to think. And time, I realized, was what I needed badly.

I mean, this was a real mind-blower. I mean, codes with figures or letters of the alphabet—all right. *They're* what *I'm* good at. Not—not these *squiggles.*

It wasn't all that warm in the McGurk basement, even with the door shut. But as I stood there, staring at the message, I began to sweat.

"Well?" said McGurk.

"Er—it does remind me a bit of cuneiform," I said, stalling.

"Uniform?" said McGurk.

"No—cuneiform," I said. "The writing—"

"—of the ancient Babylonians," said Brains, thoughtfully. "They used to stamp it on clay tablets with wedge-shaped markers. Possible, Joey. Possible. Do you happen to know how to read cuneiform?"

"No," I said. "Don't *you*?" It was a nasty crack. I

guess I was getting as irritable as the others. "Sorry, Brains!" I said. "I'm not trying to put you down. Anyway, I only said it reminded me a *bit* of cuneiform. But these are definite arrows, not just wedge shapes. . . . No."

Wanda sighed.

"How about the envelope, McGurk? Maybe the sender put his return address on the back, instead of along the top on front."

She reached out. She got a rap from the tweezers. McGurk told her not to bother.

"Nothing on the back. Just our address on front. And the stamp, of course. And the postmark."

"Ah! The postmark!" I said, reaching for McGurk's magnifying glass. "That should tell us *something.*"

"Yeah. Simply that it was posted yesterday, in this town," said Brains. "Which narrows it down to about fifty thousand people."

I ignored his remark. My interest in the postmark was just an excuse, anyway. I find it helps with codes to turn away from them sometimes—examine something completely different—then return to the code with fresh eyes. Kind of taking it by surprise.

But *this* one wasn't about to be taken by surprise.

The clock ticked away, Willie came back with his

mother's shorthand book, somebody suggested it was Chinese algebra, everybody got madder and madder, and we ended by making careful copies and going home with them, to puzzle the code out in peace and quiet.

At least that was the idea.

All over town, kids our age were enjoying themselves in the fresh snow—all through the rest of the morning and in the afternoon. Snowmen were being built. Igloos were being constructed. Slides were being slid on. Kids were out on sleds and homemade skis.

But none of this was for the McGurk Organization.

We were like the young musical geniuses you hear about. Slaving away, practicing scales and things, while other kids enjoy themselves in the fresh air.

Not that we minded.

Those dumb signs had gotten us hooked—just as if they really *were* fishhooks (one of Willie's ideas) and we were the fish.

And it wasn't until Sunday—well into the afternoon—that McGurk called to say it had been solved.

"Well—uh—halfway solved, at least."

"Who?" I gasped.

"Brains," he said. "Who else? But don't worry, Joey. There's still work to be done on it."

3 The Cracking of the Code

Brains was very smug. But who could blame him? He really had put his scientific mind to work.

"It was the arrow that set me on the right track," he said. "The big one on the left, standing on its own."

"A compass pointer?" I said. "Pointing due north? I thought of that, too."

"Good try, Joey," said Brains. "Very good. And very close." He was smiling, but he wasn't being sarcastic. He wasn't at all annoyed now. "As a matter of fact, I'd been thinking the same thing. Maybe the rest of the marks referred to directions. You know.

Starting from here. Like one block to the south, then one block east, then one block east-southeast, and so on."

"But that sounds great!" said Wanda. "Didn't you follow up on it?"

"Of course!" said Brains. "But it only led me to the middle of a vacant lot and I knew that couldn't be the place. No . . . . I suddenly realized there are more things with dials and pointers than compasses."

"Like clocks and watches," said McGurk, nodding wisely. (As if *he'd* thought of it first!) "Go on, Brains."

"I'd just happened to glance at my watch . . . ."

He glanced at it again: a huge thing, showing the time in different parts of the world, and the day and month—oh, and all sorts of things that a guy like Brains should be expected to know in his head anyway.

"But watches have numbers," said Willie.

"Not all of them," said Wanda, showing her own. It was marked with little black ticks instead of numbers. "I'm beginning to see—"

"So if the big arrow on the left is supposed to be the minute hand pointing to twelve," said Brains, "the rest is easy. These just have to be hour hands.

So—the first points to *six*, the second to *nine*, the third to *eight* . . . ."

I was busy jotting these figures down. By the end of Brains's explanation, we had this:

"Which is where *you* come in, Joey," said McGurk. "Find out the letters the numbers stand for and we have the name of the client."

I was already working on it. If A = 1, B = 2, and so on, we would get—what?

I scribbled away, rapidly at first, then slower and slower.

FIH ICFC?

It just didn't make sense.

Nor did any other combination, like when I made B = 1, C = 2, and so on.

GJI JDGD?

No way!

I'd covered pages and pages with numbers and letters, praying the first three would come out as JIM or TOM or SAM—and show we were getting there—before Wanda and Willie (of all people!) hit on the true solution.

"Even if we got the name," said Willie, "how would we know where he lives?"

"It might be someone we know," said Wanda.

"Yeah, but if it *isn't*?"

Wanda shrugged.

"Well, first thing I'd do is look in the phone book. If—*Hey! Wait a minute!*" She was flushed now. Her

eyes sparkled as she stared at the numbers. *"Of course!"* she yelled. "That's it! We have it already! It isn't a name. It isn't an address. It's a *phone number*! A real one at that!"

McGurk shot out of his rocking chair like it was a fighter plane's ejector seat. I thought at first he was going to hug Wanda. But no. He zoomed straight past her to the bottom of the stairs leading up into the house.

"Come on, men!" he cried. "My folks are out. Let's call right now!"

Less than a minute later, we were all crowding around the phone in the McGurk hallway. He'd dialed the number and we could hear the phone ringing at the other end. Then there was a click and we heard a man's voice.

"Yes?"

"This—this is Jack P. McGurk. Of—of—"

"Of the McGurk Organization, right?"

"Right!"

"Well, I must say it took you long enough! Can you come over right away? I'm staying at . . . ."

My hand was trembling as I took down the address. Not with fear so much as excitement. Though later—when we were up to our necks in the case—

But slippery though the case turned out to be (as slippery as the ground outside!) let's just take it one step at a time.

And *our* next step was going to see the new client.

4 The Spy

"Why, this is Doctor Hart's house!" Brains said, when we reached the front gate.

McGurk frowned at the address.

"Well this *is* the place," he said. "Only the guy gave his name as *Fitch*." He glared at me. "You sure you took it down right?"

I glared back.

"It's the name and address you repeated back to him, to double-check."

Brains grinned.

"Hey! That's O.K., fellas. I only said it's Doctor Hart's *house*. But he's gone on a special six months' leave to Paris and he's renting out the house while he's over there."

We opened the gate and trudged up the driveway. It was still thick with the latest snow. Only a single pathway had been cleared, and that was beginning to crumble at the edges.

"Looks like no one comes and goes much," said Wanda.

"Hm!" murmured McGurk, as we reached the front door. "I hope it's not just a trick to get us to come and shovel snow for him."

"*You* should know about tricks like that, McGurk," said Wanda. "Ring the bell and let's find out."

For a few seconds after McGurk had pressed the bell, there was no response. Then, just as McGurk was getting ready to ring again, a voice called out:

"I'll be right there. Hold on."

This was followed by a strange thudding noise.

Clump! Clump! Clump! . . .

Faint at first, then louder, then stopping behind the door.

The door opened.

"Hi!"

A tall man. Thick white wavy hair and a thin brown face. His eyes were a clear blue: rather small

but very steady. He was wearing a blue open-neck shirt and blue denim jeans. The left leg of the jeans had been cut off way above the knee. This was because the rest of the leg was in a plaster cast. He was leaning on a pair of aluminum crutches. We now understood the reason for his slowness and for the noise.

"O.K.," he said. "Come on in and close the door after you." He clumped back down the hallway and we followed. "And don't worry," he said, over his shoulder. "I'm not going to ask you to clear the snow."

McGurk gasped and glanced at me—partly shocked, partly puzzled. After all, he *had* only murmured his remark, in a very low voice.

"And whoever said this is Doctor Hart's house was quite right," said the man, standing to one side to let us into one of the rooms. Except he's on leave in Zurich, Switzerland—not Paris, France."

"But—but—"

Brains was staring up at the man like he'd not only seen but also *heard* a ghost.

"Yes, son?"

"But—I said all that out *there*! Down at the end of the driveway. You couldn't possibly have heard me."

"Couldn't I?"

The man smiled grimly. He waved one of his crutches around at the chairs and sofas and things in the well-furnished room.

"Take a seat, everybody."

We all sat down on the long sofa, side by side, right at the edge. The man himself went and sat at a desk near the window. There was a typewriter on the desk and a stack of paper. Among other things.

"Lip reading?" said McGurk, leaning farther forward and glancing at the window.

The man smiled.

"You must be McGurk," he said. Then he shook his head and reached for one of the objects on the desk. "No. The window looks out on the back yard. *This* is what I used."

Willie gave a little yelp—and no wonder. The whole Organization had stiffened. The man had picked up what looked like a gun.

It had a trigger, anyway.

But then we realized the barrel was too wide and was blocked at the end with some dark material. And there was a wire leading from the part near the trigger, with a small plug at the end. The man stuck the plug in his ear, squeezed the trigger and slowly moved the "gun barrel" in different directions.

"Hey!" cried Brains. "That's a listening device! A directional electronic listening device!"

"Correct!" said the man. He took out the plug and put the device back on the desk. "Good for up to two hundred yards out in the open. About a fifth of that through walls. Almost obsolete now, but still effective. Sit down."

The last remark was to Brains.

"But can't I just *hold* it?" pleaded our crime-lab expert. "I'm interested in science and—"

"I said sit down," the man repeated, in a low but very crisp voice.

Brains told me afterward that that was the first moment he realized there was something not very nice about Mr. Fitch.

I know how he felt because it was my turn next.

The man asked if we had any identification.

"Sure!" said McGurk, pulling out his ID card. "Take a look, sir!"

And he ordered the rest of us to show ours.

Well, at first I thought what a great guy Mr. Fitch was, after all. I mean, I'd slaved away at typing those ID cards and this was the first person who'd really *studied* them. Every word, every detail, glancing up from time to time to look at us as we stood there in front of his desk.

"Good," he said, after about five minutes.

"I typed them," I said, proudly.

"I designed them," said McGurk.

"*This* is dumb, though," said Mr. Fitch, tapping one of the cards. "Giving the age of the holder in years, months and days. That was only good for the day the card was made out. You're all a bit older now." He smiled. "What you should have put was simply the date of birth."

McGurk gulped. He gave me a quick glare.

"Yes, sir. Sure. That *was* dumb, Joey. You'd better fix it. A complete set of new cards."

I felt too mad to reply.

And that was the moment *I* first took a dislike to the man—ex-Government Secret Agent or not!

Yes. That's what he told us he was.

"I'm off the active list," he explained. "Retired a couple of years ago. And now"—he nodded toward the typewriter and pile of paper—"I'm writing my memoirs . . . ."

We listened carefully, almost openmouthed. I mean, it isn't every day you meet a real spy, even an ex-spy. And his listening device seemed to prove he was what he said.

"So where do we come in, sir?" asked McGurk.

"I'm getting to that," said the man. "I'm doing my writing here, in this town, not just for the peace and quiet. I'm doing it here because an old colleague of mine—another retired agent—lives here. He—let's just call him X—he never was very friendly, but we had a lot of respect for each other. Had to, with our lives at stake, working undercover in East Germany and Korea and places like that. . . . Anyway, I need his help again. Checking facts, comparing notes. But this time he isn't so eager to give his help—on account of this is a *private* project of mine."

Mr. Fitch sighed.

"I've had to promise him a cut of the profits from the book. And even then he's been very iffy. Wants to be sure I'm still in his league, he says. So"—he sighed again—"he insists on this dumb test."

"Test, sir?"

McGurk's eyes were glowing. Plenty of respect *there.*

"Yes. Test. To see how good I am at pickups and drops mainly. Not to mention codes."

"Pickups and drops?"

"Yeah. Like when we were in enemy territory. We had to arrange how to pick up messages and drop replies without being found out. Secret hiding places, places normal folks would never dream of looking. So X wants to make three drops, in this town, giving me the location of each one in code—the code for the next location to be the message that's dropped. If you follow me."

"Like a treasure hunt, sir," said Wanda. "Trees are good places to—"

"Exactly!" said Mr. Fitch. "A treasure hunt. With the reward for picking up the three notes to be X's cooperation with the book. The fool!"

"What about the *drop* part?" I asked. "What are you supposed to leave in place of the message?"

"Good question. Answer: the last message, with the code duly cracked and initialed. In a real operation, of course, it would be money maybe, or further requests or instructions. Anyway"—he slapped the thick plaster on his left leg—"it would have been a cinch except for this."

"Did you fall and break it in the snow, sir?" asked Wanda.

"No. On a patch of oil in the garage. Weeks ago. But I could get around fine with my crutches—before the snow."

We murmured our sympathy. Trying to get around on crutches with snow on the ground would almost certainly have meant another nasty fall and break.

"But wouldn't—er—X postpone the test?" asked Wanda. "Until the snow has cleared?"

Ex-Secret Agent Fitch laughed nastily.

"You don't know that guy, honey. I tried it—sure. But all he said was: 'You think a busted leg would have gotten you a postponement on a real operation?' He's right, too."

"But how *would* you have managed?" asked Wanda. "On a real operation, I mean?"

"The way I'm going to manage now. By recruiting local help. Reliable local help. And the most reliable local help in enemy-occupied territory was the resistance movement. Often kids like yourselves—smart kids—"

"Gee!" said McGurk.

He said it for all of us. We simply *loved* the idea of being resistance workers, helping a friendly spy.

Then we stiffened again when Mr. Fitch went on, grimly:

"—*willing to risk their lives.*"

Our faces must have given us away. He laughed.

"But there's no such risk here, of course. *Although*"—he became serious again—"you'll need to act like there was. Because if you blow it—just one single pickup or drop—I don't get the cooperation I need from X. And you don't get your fee."

"Don't worry about that, Mr. Fitch," said McGurk. "The Organization's never let anyone down yet. How did you hear of us, by the way?"

"The cleaning lady. I told her I needed a bunch of smart kids to run errands."

"When do we start?"

The ex-spy looked pleased at McGurk's readiness.

"The first pickup is tomorrow. Four-thirty in the afternoon. Not a second earlier, and as soon after that as possible. You never can be sure someone won't stumble across the package by accident."

"Package?" said Willie.

"Yes. Whatever is used to wrap the message in. This kind of weather it'll have to be waterproof, naturally."

"Naturally," said McGurk. "So where—?"

"Ah, now *that* is still to be figured out," said Mr. Fitch. He opened a desk drawer and took out a piece of paper. "He sent his first note—the starter—by ordinary mail. All the rest will have to be picked up at the drops." He waved the paper. "It's in code. I want you to take it away and work on it and report to me at 3:30 tomorrow afternoon. I'll probably crack it myself before then—but I'll still need your knowledge of the local area to pinpoint the place. And your legs, of course, to do the picking up and dropping."

"Excuse *me!*" said McGurk. He just beat Brains to the desk. He practically snatched the paper from the man. "Maybe we can—uh—crack it—uh—right . . . now . . . ."

His voice had trailed off—and not surprisingly.

For here's what was written down—this time in longhand:

W^m eau
edeighl
ove
ceedown
ghiti

5 Willie "Laffs" Last

This chapter ought to be written in that fancy scroll-type lettering. Something very special. Because it was *I* who cracked that code—

𝔦, 𝔍𝔬𝔢𝔶 ℜ𝔬𝔠𝔨𝔞𝔴𝔞𝔶.

With a little help from Willie.

It happened like this . . . .

None of us had gotten anywhere at all with the code until 10:15 the following morning. That was in school, during our English lesson. There were some pretty bleary eyes in the McGurk Organization by then, I can tell you. Most of us had lain awake half the night, grappling with the problem. McGurk himself had even told me he was relying on Mr. Fitch to crack the message himself.

"After all, he was *trained* for the job," he said.

But I couldn't give in so easily. I mean, my reputation as the Organization's word expert was at stake. And I didn't want Brains to beat me to it again.

Then, at 10:15, it happened.

"Oh, dear!" said Miss Williamson, bending over Willie's shoulder. "How many times do I have to tell you, Willie? You don't spell *laugh* l-a-f-f."

Willie looked up.

"Huh?"

McGurk guffawed.

"Dummy!" he said.

"I heard that, Jack McGurk," said Miss Williamson. "And since you find laughing itself so easy, let's see if you can spell the word." She handed him a stick of chalk. "Write it. On the board. The word *laugh*."

McGurk shrugged. After what he'd been wrestling with for the last eighteen hours, this must really have seemed a pushover.

He got it right, too.

"Fine," said Miss Williamson. "Your spelling, I mean. Your manners are something else. Don't you know how rude it is to laugh at someone else's mistake?" She turned to Willie. "Besides, there's nothing to be ashamed about. It's all the fault of the silly way the English language is spelled in many cases."

Willie brightened up.

"You just have to work at it and learn most of the words by heart," the teacher went on.

Willie slumped.

"Can anyone give me another example of the letters *gh* making an *f* sound?" asked Miss Williamson.

Several hands shot up, including mine.

"Joey?"

"Cough," I said.

"Good!" said Miss Williamson, writing it on the board.

Then someone else offered *tough* and McGurk made up for his bad manners with *rough*.

"But *gh* doesn't always come out as *f*, does it?" Miss Williamson continued. "Right, Sandra?"

"No, ma'am," said Sandra Ennis. "There's *sleigh*."

"*Very* good!" said the teacher, writing it on the board. "And very topical. . . . Wanda? Do you have another example?"

"Yes, ma'am," said Wanda, giving her old enemy a dark look, still remembering the Treetop Treasure case and Sandra's part in it. "Bough!"

"Wow!" I cried.

Well, the class broke up. I mean, it came out like a dog's bark—Wanda's "bough" and my "wow."

"Come right up here, Joseph Rockaway!" said Miss Williamson. "And apologize. To me. To Wanda. And the class."

"Sorry, Miss Williamson," I mumbled. "Sorry, Wanda. Sorry, class."

I must have looked properly downcast, because

the teacher let it go at that. But inside—man!—I was bubbling, jubilant, overjoyed.

Because my cry of "Wow!" hadn't been clowning at all. It had just spilled out because I had suddenly found the key to the code.

It still needed work, of course. But by 3:15 I had it.

"Take the word *edeighl*," I said, when we'd assembled in McGurk's basement. "That was the one I got first."

"Well?"

The others looked blank.

"Or at least the end of it: *eigh* followed by *l*. If you pronounce that *eigh* as in *sleigh* or *eight*, what do you get?"

"Uh—*ail*?" suggested Wanda.

"Right!" I said.

"But *edail* isn't a proper word either," said Brains.

"No," I agreed. "So I looked closer at that *ed*. Very common combination. It comes at the end of words like *placed* and *faced* and *passed*. Right?"

They nodded, still looking puzzled.

"But you don't pronounce those words *play-sed* and *fay-sed* and *pass-sed*, right? No. You say place-*t* and face-*t* and pass-*t*. Which makes that *ed* at the front of *eighl* or *ail* into a *t*."

"Hey! *Tail!*" cried McGurk.

"Right! And after that the rest is easy. Like *ove*. Pronounce it as you do in *love* or *shove* or *shovel* and you get—"

"*Of!*" cried Brains.

"Right again!" I said. "Now in the very next word we get that *ed* again. Make it a *t* and we have *ce-town.*" I wrote it down. "Still no such word? O.K. But treat that *ce* as you would in *place.*"

"And you get an *s,*" said Wanda. "Which makes—uh—*stown?*"

She pronounced it like the *frown* she was wearing.

"Yes," I said. "But if you pronounce *own* like you do in the phrase *my own*—you get *stone.*"

"Go on!" whispered McGurk, his eyes gleaming. "So far we have *tail of stone. Stone what?*"

"Hold it!" said Brains. "The *gh* in the last word, *ghiti*. That's pronounced *f*—correct?"

"Yes," I said.

"As in *laugh*," murmured Willie.

"So?" said Brains. "*Fiti*? What kind of a word's that?"

"No kind," I said. "Until you pronounce *iti* the way you do in *initials*."

"—*ish*?" said Wanda.

"Yeah, sure!" said McGurk. "Making *fish*! Joey, you're a genius. *Tail of stone fish*." He frowned. "But what does that mean?"

"Let's get the last word out of the message. It might help us figure the whole thing out," I said, feeling very good. "Starting with that *Wm*."

"Oh, that!" said Willie. "That's short for *William*."

"Yes, right," I said. "But—what else is short for *William*?"

"Er—*Willie*?" said Willie.

"Yes. And what else?"

"*Bill*?" said Wanda.

"Good," I said. "So now we have *Bill* and the letters *e-a-u*, as in—"

"*Beautiful*?" suggested Wanda. "But that would make it—uh—*Bill-eeoo*. . . ."

"Try *beau*," I said. "As in boyfriend."

"*Bill-oh!*" shouted McGurk. "Or—*below.* Yeah!"

"So now at last we have it in full," I said, turning to the page in my notebook where I'd written it down earlier. "Like this. . . ."

Below
tail
of
stone
fish.

"What's more," I said. "I know just where to find that stone fish!"

McGurk laughed. Now *he* was bubbling.

"So do I! . . . But first we have to check with Mr. Fish—uh—I mean *Fitch.* Come on, men! It's 3:30 already."

6 The Stone Fish

Once again Mr. Fitch got me mad.

I mean, even McGurk had praised me. Called me a "genius," even. And that's like the Congressional Medal, coming from *him*!

But the ex-spy spent the first five minutes ignoring my notebook page. Instead, he lectured us for being late. A crummy ten minutes!

"In the field of operation, split-second timing is vital," he said. "If a rendezvous is arranged for a certain time, that time must be kept to. . . ."

And so on, and on, and on.

What got me madder was the way the others were drinking this in. Words and phrases like "rendezvous" and "field of operation" seemed to hypnotize them.

But finally *I* got a word in.

"It was my fault," I said. "I was explaining to them how I managed to crack the code."

Mr. Fitch nodded.

"Ah, that—yes. Not too difficult, was it? A useful rough and ready little code, especially in a non-English-speaking country. Here, of course, it isn't so safe. Every high school kid should be able to get it within an hour or so. . . . It took me just over forty minutes, I admit. But then I'm getting rusty."

Mad? I was hopping. And again what made it worse was the attitude of the others. Nodding in agreement with him, McGurk the most vigorously of all. The jerks!

"Anyway," said the ex-spy, glancing at my translation, "this is where your help becomes really important. Your local knowledge." He frowned. "What *is* this stone fish? *Where* is it? Some kind of statue?"

"You bet, sir!" said McGurk. "In back of the library. In the garden of rest. Where people sit in summer. There's a pond and this stone fish is in the center, like a big kind of salmon, leaping."

The man frowned again.

"Hm! Well, I guess the pond just has to be frozen solid enough to walk across. It isn't the sort of place *I'd* have picked, though."

You see! He was even criticizing his old partner now! No wonder X wasn't very friendly with him.

McGurk grinned.

"That pond wouldn't *ever* be a problem, sir. Even if it wasn't frozen solid. It's very shallow. And we're all wearing rubber boots or overshoes." He stood up. "Ready, men? I figure the drop will have been made in the snow, right below the tail, on that little island the fish stands on."

Mr. Fitch half rose.

"Not so fast!" He glanced at his watch. "It's only four o'clock. How long will it take you to get to the library?"

"Ten minutes, sir."

The man sat down again.

"O.K. So I want you to leave here at 4:20. No earlier."

"But," I said slowly (and a bit nastily, I guess), "you said it was important not to be late."

He gave me a sharp look.

"So I did. So you better not dawdle, had you? Once you do start." He smiled. "Besides, I want to make sure your leader here isn't tempted."

McGurk looked shocked. The freckles shot back from his widened eyes.

"*Sir?*"

"You know what I mean, McGurk. If you got there before 4:30, you'd be snooping around to see who makes the drop. Right?"

McGurk's eyes dipped.

"Well . . . ."

"Well, that would be bad. Very bad. In the first place, it could scare the operative away—and prevent the drop from being made at all. Don't forget: X is a skilled agent, and skilled agents don't like being identified by couriers."

"Couriers, sir?" asked Willie.

"Yes. Messengers, if you like."

"I like *couriers* better," said McGurk, sitting up and looking important. "Couriers . . . yeah!"

"Whatever," said the man. "The point is, X was very particular about it. On the phone this morning. When I told him I was going ahead the way I would have on a real op. Using—uh—couriers. Young resistance workers to do the legwork. 'Well O.K.,' he said. 'Just so long as they don't identify *me!*' "

McGurk growled.

"But if we did identify him—I mean on a real operation—he'd be safe. *We'd* never give him away!"

"Oh, no?" said the man. "And if the secret police captured you, you think *they* wouldn't get it out of you?"

Then he went on to tell us of agents he had known who had broken under torture.

McGurk fell very silent then. So did the rest of us.

"And even those who didn't break that way," Mr. Fitch ended, "they usually had the information *eased* out of them. With truth drugs."

"Pentothal!" whispered Brains.

"Yes," said the man, giving him an approving nod. "That and a whole lot of other kinds."

This was very fascinating. By now we had almost forgotten our mission.

Mr. Fitch didn't, though. He'd been glancing at his watch all the time.

And at 4:15 he said:

"Well—to work!"

Then he wrote out the solution—*my* solution—on the back of the original code note, and initialed it.

"Now this," he said, getting up, with the note in one hand, "is what you'll leave in place of what you pick up. To prove to him that no stranger has accidentally picked up his next message. O.K.?"

We nodded.

"Good. So I'll just go get a plastic pouch to wrap it in. . . ." He hesitated, leaning on his crutches. "And be sure you don't let anyone see *you* placing it at the drop."

"Don't worry about that, sir," said McGurk. "Uh—when will X pick it up? Soon after we drop it?"

The man gave him a hard look.

"As soon as he thinks it's safe. When you're all well clear of the area. Neither of us wants any snooping after the pickup and drop. Understood? . . . For the same reasons. . . . In fact, I want to see you

all again, *here*, by 4:45. That gives you just enough time to make the switch and get back. And that means *all* of you."

This was one very suspicious guy, all right!

But then I guess you have to be, in his trade.

Anyway, he was back in the room with the plastic bundle tightly tied and ready to go by 4:19 precisely. And at 4:20 we were on our way.

"What if it's the *wrong* stone fish?" Wanda asked, as we hurried along the slippery sidewalk.

"You know another?" said McGurk.

"No."

"Well O.K., then. And—hey—if we go a bit quicker we might get there before 4:30."

"Or break *our* legs," grunted Brains.

But Wanda latched onto the reason right away.

"*McGurk!*" she said. "You heard what Mr. Fitch said about snooping!"

"Only kidding!" said McGurk, steadying himself as he went into a skid, and then slowing his pace a little. "Except torture wouldn't break *me*. Or truth drugs."

"Oh, no?" said Willie. "Not even the truth drugs?"

"No. I'd get Brains here to fix an antidote. A little capsule to break under my tongue. Then no matter how much Pentagon they pumped into me—"

"Pentothal," said Brains. "The drug's called Pentothal."

"—it wouldn't work," said McGurk, his eyes gleaming happily.

By the time we reached the library, there was less than a minute to go to 4:30.

"Now just act natural," said McGurk, as we made our way through the parking lot. "Let's—uh—yeah! Let's stage a snowball fight and work around to the garden gradually."

We did this—yelling and hurling and ducking and dodging—just like any regular bunch of kids having fun in the snow.

The garden was deserted. It was a murky afternoon—gray and dismal. No one else was around. Or *seemed* to be, anyway.

That thought—and the sight of the stone fish rearing up in the center of the pond—put a brake on our horseplay.

Then:

"See that!" whispered McGurk.

He was pointing to a line of footprints going across the snow-covered ice of the pond. They went close to the statue, then on past it to the other side. Large prints, some of them clear enough to show a special pattern.

Later, I drew that pattern from memory. It was to become a very important clue, so I might as well show a sample here:

But what struck us at the time to be more important than that pattern were the sliding marks.

I mean every so often a break in the regular prints and a long sliding mark.

"I bet he was pretending to test the ice," said McGurk, staring thoughtfully at these marks.

This made us suddenly aware of X as if he'd been present. We glanced around. The garden was still deserted apart from us, but there were bushes everywhere—thick evergreens, still loaded with snow.

And, over from the parking lot: footsteps and voices every so often, with the slam of car doors and the starting of engines. Somehow—in the circumstances—creepy.

Then McGurk insisted on continuing the snowball fight.

"Come on, Joey! You and me against the rest! Let's take cover behind the fish there!"

We scampered across the pond, over the footprints, in a thickening shower of snowballs.

It was a fierce shower, too. Wanda and the others were a bit too realistic with some of their shots. I guess they were miffed at being left out of the actual pickup. In fact, I had to throw back pretty hard myself to fend them off, and I didn't get much help from McGurk. He was bending under the fish's tail,

grunting, pretending to make snowballs for me,
while really groping around for the package.

Then:

"Got it!"

I glanced down. He was scraping snow off a plastic package identical to the one we'd brought along.

"Quick!" I said. "Shove it in your pocket. And

hand me our own package. *I'll* plant it. It isn't like you to do all the snowball-making while I do the throwing. Anyone who sees it will get suspicious."

He had to agree.

With another grunt, he handed over our own package. Then I did the stooping and pretending to make snowballs.

I thrust the package as deep in the snow as I could—which wasn't very far, after all the scraping and scooping McGurk had done. Most of the snowballs I did make went to cover the package further.

Finally, I said, "That should do it."

"O.K., men!" McGurk called out. "Let's play some —*chug*—"

The *chug* wasn't a word, not even in code. It was a sound. The sound of a plump well-aimed snowball from Wanda hitting him full in the mouth.

So there was nothing playful or phony about the running snowfight we had all the way back to Mr. Fitch's. It even made us late again. All of six minutes.

But he cut short his lecture, when McGurk handed him the package.

"Uh—I'll be right back," he said, clumping out of the room with it. "He tied it so tight I'll need a knife."

"Use mine, sir," said Brains, holding out his Swiss Army knife—an object almost as wonderful as his watch, bristling with gadgets.

But Mr. Fitch was already through the door.

When he came back, it was with a new code message.

"Hm!" he murmured, smoothing it out on the desk. "This looks a bit more intricate. See what you can make of it. No—not now. As soon as I've made a copy for myself, take it away with you and report to me at the same time tomorrow—3:30. And don't be late, this time, whether you manage to solve it by then or not!"

We were already puzzling over it as we went down his driveway.

Intricate?

Well, at first sight it didn't look at all bad. I mean, there was even an address in plain writing at the top. But then—

Here it is. In full.

Mr A.L.
123 Gettysburg Avenue

6, 10, 3, 24, 32, 31,   52, 11
24, 52, 10, 11, 31,   6, 10, 31, 5
31, 32, 4, 2, 10, 31   31, 10, 1, 31
10, 15, 9, 11, 3, 9.

7 McGurk Makes a Speech

Luckily, there was no school the following day. The fuel had run out and there was no heat. We had been told the day before to stay home and do some work there. Background reading and stuff like that.

I say "luckily" because without that extra time we might never have cracked the latest code. And although Smartypants Fitch would probably have told us he'd worked it out inside ten minutes, I for one wouldn't have liked to go there at 3:30 and confess failure.

What is more, don't anyone dare say we were cheating on our school by working on the Organization's business instead of reading. I mean, tackling that code was much tougher than regular school-work. It involved:

English;

Math;

Geography; and

History.

Yes. History. Especially history. I guess you could throw in a little science for good measure, too.

The English and math were basic, of course. We had to translate those numbers into letters somehow. Letters that joined up into words that made sense. So as soon as we got back to McGurk's basement that evening, I said:

"Right! . . . It looks like we'll have to do it the hard way, the scientific way."

"Oh?" said Brains.

"Yes," I said. "Starting with A = 1, B = 2, and so on. Then if that doesn't work, letting A = 2 and B = 3, and so on. And," I said, "if you think I'm going to do that all on my own, right through to X = 1, Y = 2, Z = 3, and so on—you can forget it."

"How's that?" said McGurk.

"We split the assignment. There are twenty-six letters in the alphabet. We'll take five each, which makes twenty-five, and I'll take the extra one myself. I'll work on A, B, C, D, E, and F—letting each equal one and like that. McGurk, you work on G through K. Wanda, L through P. Willie, Q through U. And Brains, you take the rest."

"But some of these numbers go up to 52," said Wanda.

"That's right," said Brains. "Which means we'll have to keep on going after 26. Say the last letter you come to is A—like if you started with B = 1. Then you'll have to keep going with B now becoming 27 and C, 28. And so on."

His eyes were shining. The more complicated a thing gets, the better Brains likes it. I even suspect he had ideas for working it out on some homemade computer.

Well, if he had, it was a failure. Because when we all met up again next morning he was just as bleary-eyed as the rest of us.

"I think we're not paying enough attention to that ordinary address at the top," he said. "Are you all *sure* there's no Gettysburg Avenue in this town?"

"Positive," I said.

"Well, I've a good mind to go to the library and check with the town street plan," he said.

"You do that, Brains," McGurk said wearily. "And check on the towns nearby, while you're at it."

Brains was back within the hour. There was no

need to ask him how he'd done. His face said it all.

The rest of us were busy rechecking our rows of letters and figures.

"You'd better go through *yours* again," I said to Brains.

Then McGurk suddenly gasped.

We turned, hopefully.

He'd grabbed the piece of paper and was staring at it as if the ink had changed color or something.

"Well . . . how about *that*?" he said slowly.

"What?"

"The spot!" he said. He stabbed a finger at the page. "The grease spot here!"

We stared, with him.

"What about it?" I asked.

" 'What about it?' " he yelped. "It's the same kind as the one on the very first message. The one *he* sent through the mail to *us*! Look—"

He reached for one of the cartons we use as files: the one marked LATEST MYSTERY: RECORDS AND CLUES. He took out the only thing in it—that first message with the clock-numeral code—and laid it side by side with the new one.

He was right.

The two grease spots were in exactly the same po-

sition on the pages. The only difference was that the latest one was smaller.

"It must have been a greasy crumb on the stack of paper," said Wanda. "That's what happens. The grease goes through several pages. So what?"

"Yeah!" said Willie, before McGurk could reply. "There was one on yesterday's note, too. You must all have been too busy working on the code to notice it. But *I* did."

"Huh!" growled McGurk. "So why didn't you *say* something?"

Willie shrugged.

"No point. I sniffed at it and *still* couldn't get a whiff of anything. This cold."

McGurk glared at him.

"The smell has nothing to do with it, dummy! The fact that the spot's there at all is enough."

"Huh?"

Now we were all staring questioningly at Mc-Gurk.

"Sure!" said our leader, beginning to rock. "It means Fitch himself wrote the last two code notes—*not* this X guy."

"But"—Wanda was nibbling her lip—"couldn't the grease spots have come from his fingers when he handled the notes? Some ointment, maybe?"

"In exactly the same spot, three times running?" jeered McGurk.

"You're right, McGurk," said Brains. "It's too big a coincidence."

"Besides," said Willie, "it's the same kind of paper. The one he wrote to us on and the one X is supposed to have sent. Look!"

He was holding both sheets of paper up to the light. The watermark was clear: a ship in full sail.

We were all convinced now. The man had been deceiving us.

"And remember how he had to go out of the room both times," said McGurk. "Once to fix our package. The other to open the package we'd picked up. He didn't want us to see what *really* went in."

"Or came out," muttered Brains.

"The notes never *were* in the packages," said McGurk.

"What *was* in them then?" asked Wanda, in a hushed voice.

"Something illegal, that's for sure," growled McGurk.

Then Willie said something that silenced us all.

"Hey! *Drugs?*"

McGurk's eyes were gleaming.

After a while, he said:

"I never did like the looks of him."

"What—what do we do next?" asked Brains. "We've no *proof* it's drugs."

"Not yet," said McGurk, grimly. He looked around at us, fierce-eyed. "So we go along with him for a bit. But *today* we take a look in the package he gives us to drop. *And* in the one we pick up."

Wanda frowned.

"But—is that honest?"

"Sure it is!" snapped McGurk. "Is tricking a bunch of kids into doing something illegal—is *that* honest?"

Wanda nodded, satisfied.

Then Brains cleared his throat.

"McGurk—"

"Yeah?"

"Just one thing."

"What?"

"Before we go along with him, we have to crack the code—remember?"

"Well, it isn't essential," said McGurk. "He'll be quick to tell us what it says himself, if we fail. But—yes—I guess it'll help make him think we're still fooled if we do sweat out the answer."

"*If!*" said Wanda. "I mean, what if this Gettysburg address is in a town *miles* away, and—"

"Hey! Hold it!" cried Brains. "That's it! That's the key!"

"What is?" I said.

" 'Gettysburg Address'! Don't you see? It isn't an ordinary *postal* address. It's *the* Gettysburg Address. The one Abraham Lincoln gave. The *speech.*"

"Yeah," I murmured, taking another look. " 'Mr. A. L.' Abraham Lincoln."

"So?"

McGurk was looking annoyed. For a minute, we'd lost him.

"So I bet the numbers refer to the letters in the words of the speech," said Brains. "Sure! That's why it's 123 Gettysburg Avenue. . . . Let's go to the library and get a book on American history and—"

"Don't bother!"

McGurk had caught up. More than caught up. He'd even overtaken us.

The rocking chair swung wildly as he jumped up out of it and onto the table. Then he stood with his legs spread apart and his head in the air and his right hand on his chest.

"I know it by heart," he said. "Remember, Joey? The camp concert last year? My contribution? . . . So you take it down in your notebook while I recite."

He began well enough.

" 'Fourscore and seven years ago . . . .' "

Then he stopped. He frowned. But not for long. Suddenly his face cleared. He jumped off the table and went to the Movie Make-Up Kit in the corner— the one we sometimes use for disguises. Two minutes later he was back on the table with a bushy old beard on his chin.

"Can't do it without this," he explained.

Then, in a booming voice, he began again.

And blow me down if that guy *didn't* know the speech by heart. He knew it so well that I had to ask him to slow down some, as I scribbled away. He did get into a little difficulty toward the end—but we really only needed the words up to letter #52, which comes in the first sentence. And here is the essential part of that sentence, as I copied it out from my notebook onto plain paper, with the words well spaced out. This made it easier to number the letters clearly, the way Brains suggested. And it made the decoding a cinch—at last.

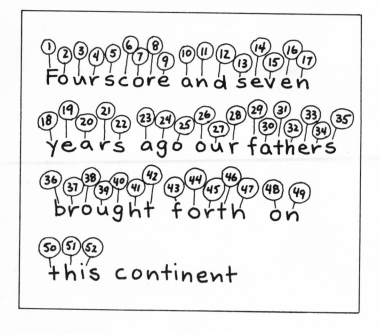

8 The Giant Cat

It didn't take long. Word by word, it came out. First *Caught*, then *in*, then *giant*, then *cat's* (which was where we began to look at each other doubtfully), then *throat*, then *Taft Avenue*.

"Caught in giant cat's throat Taft Avenue?" murmured Wanda, staring at the words in my notebook. "You sure that's right?"

"Positive," I said. "Don't forget the last message. It turned out to be a riddle, too. Even when we'd decoded it."

"Yes, but—a giant *cat*?" said Brains. "Another statue, McGurk?"

McGurk frowned.

"None that I know of. Unless it's tucked away in someone's yard."

"How about a *real* cat?" said Willie, brightly. "An *overweight* cat? *Overfed?* With a collar around its neck and the package tied to the collar? That's like its throat—uh—isn't it?"

It was a good try. For Willie. But dumb.

I mean, who'd risk a *moving* drop. Fat or not, that cat wouldn't just *sit* there, waiting for spies and resistance workers to tie and untie packages on it. And in the *snow?* Not if I know anything about cats.

I started to tell Willie this, but McGurk cut me short.

"It's still only 11:30," he said. "And there's really only one way to solve the problem. Let's take a walk along Taft Avenue."

Now Taft Avenue is very long. It leads out of town to the main highway entrance. In the center of town the avenue is naturally very busy, very crowded. But as you get toward the highway end it becomes a lot quieter. Busy with traffic, yes—but with fewer and fewer houses and stores. That's because it runs at the side of the industrial area. The factories stand well back from the avenue, beyond a high grass bank. Also screening the factories (whose entrances are way over on another road) are rows of billboards, each perched at an angle on top of the bank.

This was the end McGurk decided to start at. Afterward, he said it was a hunch. But I know McGurk better. He'd decided to start there because it was easier. Not so many houses, stores, people, etc.

Anyway, it was the *right* decision, as it happened. Because we hadn't been walking long before Wanda stopped and said:

"Aha! *There* it is!"

"The giant cat!"

She was pointing to a billboard, about fifty yards ahead. It was advertising cat food. It showed a huge red and white striped cat, head and shoulders view, looking indignant, next to a can of the food. As if to say: "Well, don't just stand there. *Open* it!"

"So what's it mean: *caught* in the cat's throat?" said Willie.

"It's got to mean *behind*," said McGurk, his eyes gleaming like the cat's. "Yeah," he said, as we drew nearer. "There's no tear in the paper where a package might be stuck. So it's got to be behind the billboard. Just about where the cat's throat appears at the front."

"Under a crossbeam, maybe," said Brains. "Taped there. Shall we look now? See if it's been—uh—dropped?"

McGurk grabbed him by the shoulder.

"No chance! Look. Nobody's been up *there*. Not yet, anyway."

The bank was smooth with drifted snow. The only marks on it were from a light spattering of slush—thrown up by the cars. Except for on the sidewalk, there were no footprints for as far as we could see.

"Could X have gotten to it from the other side?" Wanda said.

"That's what I plan to find out," said McGurk.

"We'll take a look from behind that billboard farther along. The one with the whiskey ad."

From behind the mammoth bottle of Scotch at the top of the bank, we had a good view of the back of the cat billboard. The snow was smooth there, too. We also had a good view of the factory area through a tall wire-mesh fence that ran along behind the billboards.

"That means he'll have to come to it from the Taft Avenue side, like us," said McGurk. "Yeah. But you were right about one thing, Brains."

"Oh?"

"Yes. The crossbeams behind the boards. There's one that runs straight across the middle, just about where the cat's throat is on the front side. *That's* where he'll tape the package."

There was nothing there yet, except for a powdering of snow.

"Hey, McGurk!" said Wanda. "How about staking it out? Seeing who *does* come?"

McGurk's eyes narrowed, glittering. He was tempted, I could tell. But then he shook his head.

"No. . . . Two reasons . . . . *One*: we need to see what he's really dropping. So we don't want to risk scaring him off. And *two*: you can bet the drop won't be made before 3:30. That's why Fitch is so strict about us being there at that time. Where he knows we're safely under his control. The creep!"

"Well—*after* the pickup, then?" said Wanda. "How about *then*?"

McGurk grunted.

"Maybe. I'll think about it. We still need to make sure exactly what *is* being traded, first. Until then, we can't scare them off by acting suspicious, or going against orders." He glared around at us. The steam started coming from his mouth and nose in fierce jets. "And that reminds me. When we get there at 3:30, *we act natural.* Got that? As if we still believe every word of his story. We just *have* to get a look inside those packages, men. That's Number One top priority. Uh—*Operation Open-Up!*"

9 Operation Open-Up

Act natural?

I wish McGurk hadn't given that order. It made me, for one, feel very stiff. I found it hard to know what to do with my hands. I smiled at the wrong times and kept fumbling with my glasses. I couldn't even talk right.

It had a similar effect on the others, too. For instance, the whole time we were at Mr. Fitch's, Willie didn't say a word. He just hung around with a fixed grin on his face. Wanda tended to get restless, tugging at her hair and never sitting still for more than a couple of seconds. Brains proved to be another glasses-fumbler, like me. (Except where I kept pushing them farther up my nose, Brains kept taking them off and polishing them on his sleeve.) As for McGurk, he got *too* gabby—talking faster and a whole lot more than even *he* usually does.

But I guess the ex-spy was too confident. Too sure that he had us fooled. And of course he was more interested in the day's business than in the way we looked or acted.

I mean he even gave us a bit of praise. Faint praise—but not bad, coming from him.

"Pretty good," he said. "I thought I might have to help you out with this one. But what about this Giant Cat? Any ideas?"

Willie's grin got broader and he gave a jerky nod.

"Oh, sure!" said Wanda, flinging back her hair.

"That was easy," said Brains, polishing his glasses like mad.

"Very," I said, sliding mine back up my nose.

But all this must have been lost in the torrent of words McGurk was pouring over Mr. Fitch.

"Cat—giant cat—well naturally that was the first thing we asked, I asked, ourselves, myself, yes of course, Mr. Fitch. Giant cat on Taft Avenue?—Ha! What cat? Stone cat? Real cat? No and no again, Mr. Fitch. I said we'll take a walk along there and

see for ourselves and guess what—no—I'll tell you—
you'd never guess, holed up here, not able to get out
and all—it was a *billboard* cat. Yeah! How about
that?"

Mr. Fitch looked pleased.

"Good!" he said, when at last he could get a word
in. "Good work! And—uh—how far away would you
say this billboard was? I mean how long does it take
to get there?"

"Oh, just a little farther than the library, only in a
different direction," said McGurk. "Yeah, *defi-
nitely*," he said, giving Brains a glare, when our science expert started to butt in. "Say about fifteen
minutes, yeah, a quarter of an hour, give or take a
minute, yeah—*fifteen*."

I saw what he was doing. Actually, by taking
short cuts, the billboard on Taft was no more than a
ten-minute walk away. But this was Operation
Open-Up, and opening up a package and re-tying it
—*twice*—takes time.

McGurk's gabbiness was paying off.

"All right, all right," said Mr. Fitch wearily. "Fifteen it is, then."

He glanced at his watch.

Then, hunching himself into a more comfortable

position at the desk, *he* got gabby, giving us a long talk about how he'd once used a similar drop in East Berlin.

"Behind a poster of one of their leaders," he said, grinning.

Well, it was a good story—maybe a true one for all I know. We listened with real interest, anyway, even though we knew he was playing for time again—keeping us under surveillance until he knew X would have safely made his drop.

And, sure enough, just after 4:10, he went through the same routine as yesterday. He wrote the decoded message on the back of the code note and initialed it. Then he took it out of the room—"to get the plastic pouch," he said.

Hah! As if he couldn't have had that pouch ready, right there on the desk!

When he returned, the package was tied up securely.

And at 4:15 precisely, he sent us on our way with it.

Willie nearly blew everything, out in the driveway.

"When are you gonna open up—?"

He broke off, when Brains clamped his thick wool glove over Willie's mouth.

"Willie!" said Brains, still keeping his hand clamped firmly under that long nose. "You're always thinking of candy! You already had more than your share of the first box. I'll open up the second one just as soon as I'm ready. After all, it *is* my candy!"

We others stared. For a moment I thought Brains had gone crazy. But then he held his free hand near his ear and pretended to squeeze a trigger—and we remembered the ex-spy's listening device.

Nobody spoke for *at least* another four hundred yards.

"Good thinking, Officer Bellingham!" McGurk murmured at last. "I'd forgotten about that little gadget myself. . . . But we should be O.K. here."

We'd reached a vacant lot. Some kids had been

playing there. There were several snowmen, some old chunks of cardboard at the bottom of a makeshift slide, where the ground rose slightly—and a huge snowball, taller than any of us.

A thin icy drizzle was falling. The kids must have gone in to dry off.

"This'll do," said McGurk, leading us behind the giant snowball.

Then, with Wanda holding out her long coat like an umbrella, McGurk crouched down in its shelter and untied the package.

The knot was easy, but when he'd unraveled the plastic roll, a groan went up from some of us.

"Whatever it is, he sealed it up," said Brains.

By the second "it," he meant a long envelope, folded in half. Rather a bulky envelope, too, for only one piece of paper. But anyway a *sealed* envelope.

"I'd thought of that," said McGurk, cheerfully. He felt in an inside pocket of his coat and produced a new envelope. "Here—hold this, Brains," he said. "And keep it dry."

Then he tore open the sealed envelope.

"McGurk!" gasped Wanda. "That's a white envelope. Yours is a buff one. What if X notices it's a different kind? I mean if yesterday's was white, too?"

"So what?" said McGurk, digging cautiously into the opened envelope. "Fitch could have run out of the other kind, couldn't he? Anyway, they think we're so dumb we'd never dream of doing this. Opening the plastic pouch, maybe—but not a sealed envelope.... Ready?" he said to me.

I nodded. McGurk had warned me earlier to have my notebook handy—to record accurate details of the pouch's contents.

"Paper," said McGurk, still fumbling inside. "Small pieces—" Then his hand came out and he gasped. "Hey! It—it's money. It's—gosh—one-hundred-dollar bills! Torn in half!"

We stared at the numbers: the big white 100s and the smaller green serial numbers. We stared at the smiling faces of Benjamin Franklin (or the smiling *half* faces!) and the pictures of Independence Hall, torn clear down the bell tower.

". . . eight, nine, *ten* pieces," said McGurk. "Five one-hundred-dollar bills, torn in half!"

"But why?" said Wanda.

"Never mind that now," said McGurk. "We're wasting time. Joey—take down the serial numbers."

I was already doing this. And here is the beginning of my list:

B 3099 8629 A
L 1531399 6 A
B 06058938 A
A 00274461 A
B 004139838
B 08700931 A
E 09922329 A

That's where I had to stop and take another look.

"Hey! That's seven different numbers already. And still—uh—still three to go!" I looked at McGurk. "It isn't *five* torn in half, after all. It's *ten*. Ten halves!"

Brains was frowning.

"But that means they're useless," he said. "Unless you have the matching halves and stick them together."

"Are they real?" asked Willie.

McGurk nodded.

"Sure," he murmured. "Real used C-notes. And I think I get it—this tearing in half. It means they don't trust each other, this X and Mr. Fitch. I bet in the package we dropped yesterday there was another bunch of half bills. And I bet five of them *will* match five of these. Mr. Fitch wanted to be sure of what *he* was getting—in the package we picked up for him— before paying in full."

"But what about these *extra* five halves?" asked Wanda.

"Down payment for what we pick up today. And if Mr. Fitch is satisfied with it—whatever it is—"

"Oh, drugs! It has to be drugs!" said Brains. "This sort of money. Five hundred dollars at a time."

"Whatever," said McGurk, grimly. "But if he's

satisfied, the matching halves will go in the package he sends tomorrow. Or so he hopes!"

McGurk was looking very fierce now. Then he gave a grunt and began stuffing the torn bills into the new envelope.

"Got *all* the numbers O.K., Joey?"

I nodded. McGurk licked the flap and stuck it down. Then he folded the envelope in half and wrapped it in the pouch, tying it as he strode away.

"Come on, men," he said. "We're running late."

We were beginning to move off when he had another idea.

"Oh, and grab a bunch of those hunks of cardboard," he said. "One for each of us. I know how we can use them when we get there."

10 Caught in Possession?

It was 4:35 and starting to get dark by the time we reached the cat billboard. The traffic was fairly heavy, but there was no one else around on foot.

There *had* been, though.

"Look!" said Wanda. "Up the bank!"

She was pointing to a row of footprints in the speckled snow. Or *leg*prints—because that's what most of them were. The snow had drifted deeply in places, and whoever had walked up there must have gone in up to his knees in many spots.

Near the bottom, however, the snow lay fairly thin. The footprints there were very clear.

"The same?" asked McGurk.

I nodded. There was really no need to flip back the pages of my notebook.

"Exactly," I said.

"Let's go, then," said Wanda, starting to plunge up the bank after them.

"Wait!" McGurk had grabbed the tail of her coat. "Now that we know there's something real big going on—"

"Drugs," said Brains, nodding in a matter-of-fact way.

"Something very valuable, anyway," said Mc-Gurk, patting the pocket in which he'd got the pouchful of torn one-hundred dollar bills. "So we have to be doubly careful. That's why I said to bring these." He nodded at the bundle of cardboard pieces. "We'll take one each and start sliding down the bank on them between here and the whiskey ad. It'll look more natural."

So that's what we did. Personally, I thought it was messy, with the snow so thick. But after a couple of turns each, we began to wear a regular toboggan run and then it wasn't so bad.

By "we," I mean all except Wanda. As soon as we'd reached the top the first time and made sure the back of the cat billboard was deserted, McGurk told her to go across and check the middle crossbeam. It was only about six feet from the ground, but it meant inching sideways along the ledge formed by the bottom beam. And Wanda was, after all, our climbing expert.

The rest of us were just starting on our third slide down the bank, with me at the top and McGurk on his way back up, when Wanda called: "Got it!"

"Well, keep quiet about it then!" said McGurk, in a strained voice: half shout, half croak.

He waved at her to hurry.

Her eyes were sparkling when she reached us. The package shone dully in her hands.

"Just like you said, Brains. It was taped there."

"You got the tape?" asked McGurk.

"No," said Wanda. "I left it there, dangling. It's surgical tape so we'll be able to use it again for *our* package. Gimme, McGurk."

Reluctantly, McGurk handed over the package containing the money.

"Be sure it sticks—"

"Of course!" said Wanda. "Leave it to me."

We watched her as she edged along the bottom beam again and began to fumble with the one above her head.

"O.K.," grunted McGurk, stowing the pickup package inside his coat. "Let's get back to the slid-

ing. You never know who might be watching."

"Aren't you going to open it?" said Willie.

"Here? You've got to be kidding!" said McGurk.

With that, he lay flat on his cardboard sheet, with me after him (sitting), then Willie and Brains. We had a bit of a pile-up at the bottom (that slide was getting pretty slick) and we were just picking ourselves up when Wanda came crashing down the bank, sending Willie flying into the dirty snow that had been heaped up along the side of the road.

"O.K.," said McGurk, brushing himself off. "Let's go somewhere quiet and see just what it is they *have* been trading."

The slide had been kind of fun after all, but there were no protests as he started leading us away.

No protests from *us*, that is.

But:

"O.K., you kids! Hold it right there!"

We spun around, staring, then blinking, as a spotlight was switched on and the beam cut through the drizzly murk. It slanted from the top of a police patrol car full onto McGurk's head and shoulders. Not to mention the bulge in his coat just under the left shoulder!

That's when I felt like running.

That's when I *would* have started running, if my knees hadn't gotten all jellylike.

"Caught in possession of illegal narcotics!"

The words kept going through my head. I was sure that those cops had been staking out the place —had watched our every move, including the one McGurk had made when stowing away the package.

I saw his hand creep under his coat, then stay there very still. The spotlight was still on him as one of the cops came crunching over the snow at the side of the road.

How many years was it—the sentence for being caught in possession?

I tried to remember.

Wasn't it seven to life?

I tried to forget.

The cop was nearly upon us by now. His collar was turned up against the cold.

"So it's the McGurk Foundation!" he grunted.

My spirits sank farther.

The long lean face with the dark sideburns belonged to Patrolman Morelli—no friend of ours. I peered past him to see if his partner was Patrolman Cassidy, but we were out of luck. It was a hard-eyed stranger.

"Uh—that—that's McGurk *Organization*," said our leader, timidly.

"Whatever!" growled Morelli. "But this time your fancy title isn't going to do you any good!"

11 Top Secret!

Later, McGurk confessed to us that he nearly made the biggest mistake of his career.

"I was just going to take the package out and tell him what had happened," he said. "But he was too quick about bawling us out."

"Sliding down a bank that steep!" growled the patrolman. "Straight down onto a busy road like this. Don't you realize you might have shot right under a car's wheels? Huh? Huh? Huh?"

He gave each of us a glare.

McGurk was quick to hang his head.

"Sorry, officer," he mumbled. "I guess it *was* dumb."

"Dumb nothing!" said Wanda, angrily. "There's a *huge* barrier of snow between the sidewalk and the road!"

McGurk looked like he could have kicked her. Morelli looked like he was getting ready to book her. His hand was already fumbling at his breast pocket.

"The officer's right, Wanda," said Brains, soothingly.

"Yeah!" said Willie, with *real* indignation. "*You* almost sent me flying over it just then!"

"Oh—gosh—yes!" Now it was Wanda's turn to hang her head. "Sorry, Willie! . . . Uh—sorry, Officer Morelli!"

The cop nodded grimly.

"I should think so, too! You'd be even sorrier if one of you ended up killed or maimed for life. Now beat it—and, hey—not so fast! Pick up this cardboard stuff or I'll book you for littering."

We were only too glad to do as he said.

"Now we really *are* late," muttered Brains, as we hurried away.

"Couldn't have happened at a better time!" said McGurk, gleefully.

"Huh?"

"Sure. It gives us the perfect alibi for being late. And more time to examine *this*." He patted his pocket. "We'll tell him exactly what happened, only make it seem like the cops kept us longer than they did."

"Why do we need more time to examine that?" said Wanda. "I wouldn't know a bag of heroin from a bag of confectioner's sugar. And I sure don't like the idea of trying it out on the tip of my tongue, like in the movies."

"No, but Brains wouldn't mind, would you?" said McGurk, clapping a hand on our crime-lab expert's shoulder. "I bet he knows a million other tests, too."

"Well . . . ." mumbled Brains, blinking doubtfully.

"Anyway, let's take a peek now, same place. It's still deserted."

The vacant lot looked even more dismal by now. The drizzle had stopped, but there was a sort of yellowish murk over the place, as we crouched behind the monster snowball.

"Nobody needs a knife for *this*," said McGurk, as he rapidly untied the knots. "Though you wait until we hand it over and I bet you he makes the same excuse. Of course, with a half pound of cocaine or—"

He stopped.

There was no bulging glassine bag in there.

Just another envelope. Sealed, of course. But fairly thin.

Frowning, McGurk tore it open. His frown deepened as he pulled out the folded piece of paper. It looked like another coded message, after all.

But no.

This was a larger sheet. Folded twice. And the paper was thicker, the sort used in copying machines.

"Wow!" gasped Brains.

He'd pulled out a pencil flashlight and was shining it over the page.

It was crowded with lines and lines of very small print or typewriting, with rows of figures crammed in between each block of writing, and several tiny intricate thumbnail diagrams. The page was legal size, true, but it contained as much information as any ten pages of an ordinary book. I'd give a copy here just to prove it, if this hadn't been one piece of evidence we were forced to hand over.

I can show you what was stamped right across it, though, diagonally, in red. This:

"Yes, Brains. Like you said . . . . Wow!" I said, staring at the warning.

"What's it all about?" said McGurk, peering at the close-packed words and numbers. "It isn't in code, I know, but it might just as well be, as far as I'm concerned."

"Me too!" whispered Wanda.

"It's page two of something, whatever it is," said Willie, pointing to the number at the top.

"Big deal!" snarled McGurk. "If that's all you can—"

But Brains cut him short.

"Yes, Willie," he said, slowly, thoughtfully. "And it looks to me like page two of a summary of details about some sort of printing machine . . . . Yeah!" he said, suddenly excited, holding the paper closer to his eyes. "A copying machine! And—wow!—it says here—uh—'*capable of producing full-color copies at a cost of less than $150 per machine.*' Do you realize what that means? I mean, no wonder it's classified top secret. And—hey—look here—in writing at the bottom: '*Appendixes I and II follow on p. 3. Appendix I: Details of chemical formula relating to Model FC/1P. Appendix II: Circuit diagram of same.*'"

We gaped at each other.

"So he *is* a spy!" I said.

"Yes," said Brains, nodding gravely. "But not for a foreign power. Not dealing with nuclear plants or strategic missiles. This guy"—he tapped the paper—"our Mr. Fitch—he's an *industrial* spy. Stealing secrets from commercial firms!"

"So what do we do now?" said Wanda.

"Police?" said Willie, ending with a sneeze.

"More likely the firm's security officer," said Brains. "If we knew *which* firm."

But McGurk was shaking his head. Vigorously.

"No. No way. Not yet. We need to identify X. We need to give the police or the security officer the whole picture. And for that, men," he looked around at us purposefully, "we have to take on one more assignment. Only this time we *will* stake out the place in advance."

"But how?" said Wanda. "If Mr. Fitch gets us together again at 3:30 tomorrow? Which he surely will."

"I think I have an idea," said McGurk, stuffing the folded page back in a fresh envelope. He quickly stuck the flap down and wrapped the whole thing up again in the plastic pouch. "Come on. I want to stop off at my place. Only for a minute."

He did stop off—leaving us on the sidewalk, stamping and shivering, for more like three minutes. But he had a satisfied gleam in his eyes when he came out.

It was almost five o'clock by the time we got to Mr. Fitch's, and his face looked very grim as he opened the door. However, McGurk had been right. The story of the cop car—though causing a momentary flash of alarm in the man's cold blue eyes—soon appeased him.

"You should have been more careful, even so," he said, at the end.

"But that's just what we were doing," said Mc-Gurk. "Acting like regular kids. I mean, if the cops had seen us just snooping around the billboards, they'd ha—" McGurk broke off, grabbed for a tissue and clapped it to his nose, just in time to muffle a sneeze. His eyes were watering now. "They'd have been really sus–suspic–*shooz!*"

Another sneeze—again muffled by the tissue.

The man nodded. He looked satisfied with the explanation.

"I must be coming down with a cold!" mumbled McGurk, snuffling. He said it like: "*I bust be cobbig dowd with a code.*" The last word seemed to remind him. "What *is* the next code, Mr. Fitch?" he asked, in a clearer voice.

Just as McGurk had predicted, the spy went into the tight-knot routine. This time Brains *didn't* offer his Swiss Army knife. And as soon as the man had stumped out of the room, McGurk nudged me.

"One of *your* tissues, Joey. Hand it over."

At first I was a bit reluctant. I thought he was aiming to use it. But something in that eager green gleam of his eyes told me otherwise.

"Sure!" I said.

Then I nearly had a fit when he pulled from his pocket a small can of pepper—*and started sprinkling it over my tissue!*

"Hey!" I gasped. "What—?"

"Shush!" he hissed. "You too, Joey. You're gonna make like *you're* coming down with a cold. An excuse for being absent tomorrow when—"

He had to break off, as Mr. Fitch returned. But I'd already got the message. In fact, that's probably why McGurk picked me as a partner for what he had in mind. He knows I'm a pretty quick thinker.

Then the man produced another code message, after pretending as usual he'd taken it from the package. We avoided each other's eyes, scared of giving any sign that we knew different now.

"It's another stickler, I'm afraid," he said, smoothing it out on the desk.

We clustered around. Here it is:

458, 322, 132, 145, 380

434, 147, 100, 332, 324, 126

449, 384, 6, 403, 210

28, 7, 404, 252, 146, 455

339, 2, 442, 219

163, 378, 333, 315

348, 4, 376, 254, 237, 323, 181

271, 329, 442

441, 330

66, 5, 321, 136

389, 215, 146, 282, 283

"Gosh!" whispered Brains.

"Beauty, isn't it?" murmured the man. "Are you thinking what I'm thinking, young man?"

"Well," said Brains, "it's words, obviously. With numbers standing for letters again. But—this time—there doesn't seem to be any two numbers alike!"

"Correct!" said the man. "No repeats. Therefore no obvious patterns and groupings. The worst kind."

I was getting so engrossed in this, I forgot all about sneezing until McGurk gave out with a real scorcher, over the top of his tissue, and blew the paper across the desk.

Then I put my tissue to my nose and the pepper did the rest.

"Ah-shoo!"

Mr. Fitch grinned as he handed the paper to McGurk.

"It's a good thing tomorrow's is the last assignment. Looks like more than one of you is coming down with a cold."

McGurk nodded. His eyes gleamed (feverishly, it seemed!) above his tissue.

"Yeah!" he said. "All this fieldwork in bad weather .... Feel like—uh—the Spy Who Came in from the Cold. *A-a-SHOOZ!*"

12 Stake-Out in the Snow

Willie was miffed when McGurk told him of the plan, back at our headquarters.

"I mean I have a *real* cold. But you two guys get to do the exciting part with only fake colds!"

"But that's the point, Willie," said McGurk. "We need to be A-1 fit for the job we have to do. Fully alert, with clear keen eyes that aren't watering all the time. And noses that don't fire off *accidental* sneezes and give us away."

"Huh!" grunted Willie. "I—*ashoo!*"

"See what I mean?" said McGurk. "Mr. X would hear that at two hundred yards *without* a hearing device."

"Besides," said Brains. "I'm not sure theirs *will* be the most exciting task, Willie. If Mr. Fitch should get wind of what's really happening when only three of us turn up at 3:30 tomorrow—well!"

He pulled a face.

Wanda nodded. She was chewing her lip nervously.

"It could be nasty."

"You'll be O.K.," said McGurk. "After those sneezes Joey and I faked, he's sure to believe you. Anyway"—he tapped the piece of paper on the table —"let's get to work on the code. If we can't crack this one we'll have to show up at 3:30 with you. Then there won't *be* any stake-out."

Well, he needn't have worried. That code didn't turn out to be half as bad as it looked. Either that, or we were getting better.

Inside half an hour, Wanda had spotted the key.

"That 411," she said. "It seems to me we have another telephone code here."

McGurk's eyebrows shot up.

"Oh?"

"Sure. That's the number you call for information."

"Hey, yes!" said Brains. "So maybe these numbers

are area codes. And the first letter of the place name is the letter in the code word. Have you got a phone book handy, McGurk?"

But McGurk was already on his way, pounding upstairs. When he came back he already had it open at the area code listings.

"Great!" said Brains. "Now let's take the first number. . . ."

But it was no use. Some of the numbers in Mr. X's message weren't even listed in the area codes. And those that were just didn't make any sense when applied to the message.

Then suddenly McGurk thumped the table.

"Dummies!" he said. "We've got the right book but the wrong set of numbers! I bet you anything these are *page* numbers and—"

"Right!" I said, already getting out my notebook and pencil. "Turn to page 458 and what do we have? . . . Names beginning with—uh—U. And 322—come on, come on!—yes—N. And 132—Dawson, Davidson—all the D's. . . ."

Soon we were flicking through those flimsy pages like crazy, tearing some of them in our eagerness. Because this *was* working out. And inside another ten minutes, here's what we had:

*Under second
trash basket,
path from parking
lot to band shell.*

"Mr. Fitch was right," said Brains. "It's a beauty. You don't *need* to use the same number twice. The number for any of the U pages would have been O.K. And so on."

"Never mind *that!*" said McGurk, frowning. "What's it supposed to mean? Band shell? Parking lot? Trash basket?"

"There's only one public band shell that I know of," said Wanda. "And it's slap in the center of town. In Willow Park."

"Of course!" I said. "And there *is* a pathway leading straight to it out of the parking lot. *And* it has those fancy trash cans—like deep wire-mesh baskets on little legs—every few yards. Donated by the Rotary Club. Part of last year's anti-litter drive."

"So that's where we'll be tomorrow, Joey!" said McGurk. "At a good safe distance. From three o'clock on. Think you can borrow your dad's binoculars?"

And that's where we were the next day at three.

(Fortunately, school was still closed.) I'd brought the binoculars and we took up our position behind the trunk of a big oak tree, several hundred yards from all three key spots: the parking lot, the band shell and the second trash basket along the path.

It was a brighter day, but still very cold. I envied the people walking briskly along that path—ladies with dogs, old men swinging sticks, kids having snowball fights. At least their blood was circulating warmly, while my fingers were getting numb, holding those binoculars, and my feet seemed to be slowly turning to ice.

None of that seemed to trouble Jack McGurk, though.

Now he was on the scent, some inner fire was keeping him warm and glowing.

"*Is that a shrike?*" he kept saying aloud, whenever anyone strayed from the path, near our tree. "*Or is it a bar-tailed godwit?*"

Where he got the names of the birds from, I don't know. But it was only camouflage, anyway. What he kept saying *softly*, every time some new person stepped onto the path from the parking lot, were things like: "Wonder if this is him?"—or: "Maybe it isn't a man at all. Maybe it's this woman with the sheepdog."

And questions and statements like these were always followed by:

"Give me the binoculars, Joey. I want to watch real close when he" (or "she") "gets up to the basket."

It wasn't until 3:40 that someone stopped by that second basket. A young man with a cap with earflaps. He seemed interested in something he'd seen in the newspaper he was carrying.

"He looks too young to have been an agent with Fitch in Korea," grunted McGurk. "And all he's doing is reading that paper."

That's how McGurk—by losing interest—came to let me have the binoculars back and *I* came to be the one to spot the drop.

"His age doesn't make any difference," I said, once the binoculars were safely in my hands and I was refocusing them on the man. "That fellow-agent story was probably a lie anyway. And—*wait!*" I drawled softly.

Because I'd just spotted something sliding down the man's left pant leg, from under his long dark coat.

"What?" said McGurk. "What's happening?"

All *he* could see was the man still standing there,

holding the paper in his right hand, with his left hand deep in his pocket.

But I could see the plastic package that had slid next to his left foot, and the neat little side kick he gave it that sent it scudding into the narrow space under the mesh basket—like a hockey puck into the net.

"And that's another goal for the Rangers, folks!" I said, in my best sports commentator voice.

"You flipped out or something?" asked McGurk, as the man slowly turned and strolled back to the parking lot.

"No," I said. "I've just seen the drop."

And, keeping the man focused in the binoculars, I told McGurk what had happened.

"Good!" he said. "So now we follow him. At a safe distance. Give me the binoculars."

We didn't have far to follow "Mr. Earflaps," as we now called him. The man went into the parking lot and opened the door of a yellow Cordoba and stepped inside.

"Quick! Get the number!" I said.

We were still a fair distance away, behind another tree, but with a clear view of the car.

Slowly, McGurk began to read out the numbers and letters, while I jotted them down.

"Hurry!" I said. "Or he'll be gone before we've got it all."

But I didn't need to worry.

"That's O.K.," McGurk drawled. "He's going no place. He hasn't even started the engine. He's just opening a thermos of coffee. I guess he's settling down to watch the basket—make sure no stranger goes snooping around."

There was a bright gleam in McGurk's eyes as he handed me back the binoculars. I could guess what was coming next. This was a situation McGurk simply could not resist.

"So now we have him cold turkey," he said. "We

know *exactly* where he'll be for the next forty minutes or so. So *now* we tell the cops!"

"Fine!" I said. "But what about Fitch and—?"

"They can pick him up at their leisure," said McGurk. "We know where to find *him*. *He* isn't mobile."

"Fitch and the *others*," I said. "Brains, Wanda, Willie. What about *them*?"

"What *about* them? When we've put the cops onto this guy—made sure he's in the bag—we'll wait by the trash basket and tell the other three all about it when they arrive to make the pickup."

I could just see him: bragging, telling them it was all over, all sewed up, being obnoxious. He must have read my mind.

"Uh—we'll let them have the pleasure of handing over the latest package of torn bills to the cops," he said, grandly.

Well, it wasn't going to turn out *quite* like that.

Oh, no!

13 Lieutenant Kaspar Gets into the Act

Police Headquarters is just around the corner from Willow Park, and by 3:50 we were telling Lieutenant Kaspar about the Snowbound Spy and his friend with the earflaps.

Now there was a time when the lieutenant would have had us thrown out on sight. These days, however—since we've given him real help on more than one case—he is prepared to listen with patience. Even so, his sharp blue eyes were beginning to flit restlessly as McGurk kept bragging about how good we were (himself especially) at cracking codes. And when the cop started tugging at the gold ring on his finger, I could tell it was time to interrupt.

"What's going on really," I said, "is that the ear-flap guy is trading secrets about a copying machine for one-hundred-dollar bills. Five hundred dollars a drop in fact. I have the numbers of some here," I said, opening my notebook. "With details of the machine."

"I was coming to that!" said McGurk indignantly.

"Be quiet!" said the lieutenant, leaning forward. "Go on, Joey. The details of the machine . . . ."

I gave them to him, reading from my notes. At the mention of the machine's capability and the model number, he snapped into action.

"I believe I know the factory in question," he said. "Just hold it a minute . . . ." He reached for the phone and dialed a number direct. "The security officer there," he said, with his hand over the mouthpiece. "He's an old police colleague of mine who— Oh, hi, Bill! Leonard here." (I couldn't help smiling at the gleeful joy in McGurk's eyes at this revelation of Kaspar's first name.) "Do you have a new copying machine in the development stage? . . ."

And he went on to repeat the details I'd given him.

After a pause, his eyes widened.

"You don't *say*? Well I think you'll find someone's been doing a little copying on his own. Listen."

He told the man at the other end about our investigations—keeping it short and crisp.

"Sure!" he said, finally. "Not only can they describe the man right down to the pattern of his footprints, they have his license-plate number and know exactly where to find him. Not to mention the guy who's been masterminding it. . . ."

Another pause.

"Yeah. Well. I suggest we wait until the rest of the kids make *their* drop and this guy in the car goes to pick up his loot. Then—no? . . . Worth *how* much? . . . *Phew!*" Lieutenant Kaspar's eyes got even wider as he whistled. "I see your point, Bill. We can't risk having *that* lying around a second longer than necessary. . . . Sure! We'll have it picked up right now. And him with it."

The joy returned to McGurk's eyes. He smiled at me and gave the A.O.K. sign.

Kaspar put down the phone.

"You heard that? Seems you hit on a really big one, this time. Excuse me."

He got up and went out into the main office. He left the door open, so we were able to hear snatches of what he was saying.

"Nearest patrol car . . . yeah. Give them this number . . . *now*. . . . Yes, bring him in. . . . Then tell them to go to the—uh—second trash basket on the path to the band shell and pick up a plastic package from under it. . . . No—*under* it. . . ."

"Hey!" gasped McGurk, suddenly getting up. "*We* should be in on this! Come—"

But just then the lieutenant re-entered the room.

"Sir!" cried McGurk. "Can't *we* go along?"

"No way!" snapped Kaspar. "The car was already out there, cruising the Willow Park area. It's heading for the parking lot now. There's no time to have it stop by to pick *you* up."

"We'll go on foot then!"

"You'll stay right here! Sit down! I want to know more about this Mr. Fitch. In detail, this time."

We started to tell him, impatiently at first. But as he nodded and questioned us and made notes himself, we became more enthusiastic. After all, the Earflap man was only small fry compared to the ex-secret agent.

Then, after about fifteen minutes, there came the sound of a commotion from the outer office.

"*I want to know the meaning of this!*" came a man's voice, very loud and blustery, but with a tell-tale yelp of fright in it.

We looked at each other. There was a knock on the door.

Kaspar called out, "Come in!"

The door opened and a uniformed officer entered —Patrolman Morelli.

He blinked when he saw us—then switched his attention to the lieutenant.

"We got him, sir. He saw us coming. He tried to start the car, but the engine stalled. Then he got out and ran. Almost gave us the slip, too." Morelli smirked. "But we caught up with him quick enough —over in the bus station, in a phone booth, making a call. And he tried to get rid of—uh—*these*, on the way back to the patrol car."

Morelli held out a bunch of green paper scraps and put them on the desk.

There were five pieces. Halves of one-hundred-dollar bills.

"Joey?" said the lieutenant, much to Morelli's surprise.

I knew what he wanted. I reached for the half bills and checked them against the numbers in my notebook.

"They're all down here, sir," I said.

Kaspar was delighted.

"He was hoping to pick up the matching halves this afternoon," he said. "But this is going to nail him and nail him hard. What about the package, Morelli?"

"My partner has that, sir."

"Great! Well all we—"

"*You say he was making a phone call?*" McGurk cried suddenly, with a yelp in *his* voice this time.

"Uh—yeah," grunted Morelli, looking at the lieutenant as if to ask permission to smack this bratty kid for interrupting.

"Go on, Morelli!" said the lieutenant, suddenly looking grave himself. "You sure about this?"

"Well—uh—yeah. The phone was up to his face. He was talking fast. He couldn't have had much of a conversation, because—"

"But he *was* talking to someone?" McGurk groaned.

"Well . . . ."

"Answer the kid, Morelli. I think I see what he's getting at."

Morelli shrugged.

"Well, yes."

"Oh, *no!*" McGurk stared at the clock on the wall. "And it's *still* only 4:20. They must have been with Fitch when he got the warning call!"

"They?" grunted Morelli.

"Brains! Wanda! Willie!"

McGurk looked ready to burst into tears. I knew exactly how he felt. Our fears about Fitch suspecting something when only three of the Organization turned up were nothing compared to our anxiety over this *new* peril. When the spy heard his cover had been blown—there was no telling what he'd do.

"Come on!" said Lieutenant Kaspar. "We'd better get up there right away. . . . And alert the tactical unit," he called out to the desk sergeant, as he swept out of the office with us right behind him. "Looks like we might have a potential hostage situation on our hands!"

14 The Snowbound Spy

In the back of an unmarked police car with Lieutenant Kaspar, we took the route from the Willow Park parking lot that Brains and the others would be coming along.

If they were alive to do so.

"This Fitch," said the lieutenant. "He probably really is an ex-Government agent. Most of these industrial espionage guys are. So the chances are he kept his head. Just sent them out with an empty package. Or the package with the old code message in it, like it really *was* just a game."

We were about halfway there and it was already

4:30. There was no sign of the others. My eyes were aching from looking so hard.

"On the other hand," muttered Lieutenant Kaspar, stirring uneasily, "being an ex-Government agent could make things worse. Some of those guys have to be a little crazy to do what they do when they're at their peak. When they're over the hill, and they realize they've been caught breaking the law—by a bunch of kids yet—well, he might really take it bad."

"You—you think so?" I said.

The car was traveling at a fair speed. Not so fast that we would miss spotting the others, but swiftly enough. All the same, it was the longest journey *I* ever made.

Because if the man *had* gone crazy—what?

Would Brains, Wanda and Willie know enough to be very careful? To do whatever he ordered them to?

Or would Wanda be defiant?

Or Willie panic?

Or Brains try to be too smart for his own good?

During the next few seconds, I imagined our friends being shot, clubbed, stabbed, strangled—even gassed. And I had just gotten around to remembering that real spies carry poison capsules for if they're captured—and imagining *our* spy inviting Brains and the others to join him in a cyanide snack—when I heard McGurk say to the driver, in a shaky voice:

"We—we're almost there now. Make a left turn at this next intersection."

And *still* no sign of the others.

Well, what *had* happened?

I'll let one of the survivors tell this part. After all, they were actually there, with the spy. So here's Brains's report:

SURVIVOR'S REPORT

"It was just the usual routine at first. He'd bought our story that you two were in bed with flu and he checked our code-cracking. He even complimented us on it. Then he started yacking on about a code he'd once had to crack in Hong Kong. Just killing time, of course, as usual.

"Anyway, at last he went out of the room to get the package ready.

"And that's when the phone rang on his desk.

"That in itself gave us a scare. Wanda had taken the opportunity to step up to the desk to

look at the papers on it. Just to see if he really was writing his memoirs. She was just saying, 'Not a sign of—' when the phone rang.

"She got back to her seat just in time. He came clumping back in with a puzzled look on his face. Then, when he picked up the phone, that look changed. Real alarm.*

" 'What?' he said. 'After *you?* Who? What are you talking about? Get a hold on yourself, man!'

"I was craning forward, trying to hear the other voice. It was nearly loud enough. Loud enough to hear it was a panicky voice, kind of yelpy . . . . Then—click! I distinctly heard the other person hang up.

"'Hello! Hello!' says Fitch—looking panicky himself. And he wasn't the only one. Willie hadn't caught on yet, but both Wanda and I were beginning to realize what had happened. Wanda was already on the edge of the sofa, giving me a 'shall-we-make-a-run-for-it?' look.

"Then Fitch got himself under control. Still holding the phone—his knuckles were white, though—he managed to look calmer and pretended someone was still on the line.

"'Oh, hello, Jane?' he said. 'Thank goodness, you've come. I couldn't make any sense out of Joe. Now—what was he trying to tell me? . . .'

"This was all baloney. I was still leaning forward and could hear that that line was dead. But Fitch was still taking us for dummies. Putting on his last big act.

"'What?' he said again—although not as shocked this time. 'A heart attack? . . . You sure? . . . Of course I'll be there as soon as I can. I'm leaving right away.'

"*Then he put down the phone and turned to us.*

"*'That was bad news,' he said. 'My father. He's very sick. I have to go to him right away. No more time for our little game, I'm afraid. Maybe we'll return to it later. Meanwhile, here's your money. The fee I promised.'*

"*He'd been fumbling in his wallet. Now he tossed fifteen dollars onto the desk.*

"*'And here,' he said, holding out another bunch of bills. 'Here's another twenty if you'll do me a favor.'*

"*'What favor?' said Wanda, looking at him hard.*

"*'Clear the driveway of snow. And a path from the front door to the garage. You'll find shovels and brooms in the garage. It isn't locked. But hurry! I'll be packing. If you can have it done in ten minutes there'll be an extra ten dollars for you. A dollar a minute. I've just got to catch the next flight to Chicago!'*

"*Well, I felt Wanda stiffen and I thought she was going to refuse and call him a liar. So I stood up and took charge.*

"*'Right away, Mr. Fitch,' I said. 'Come on, you two!'*

"I mean, it was simply a case of doing any-thing—anything to get out of that house.

"But of course it didn't turn out like that."

You bet it didn't! (This is me, Joey, again.)

When our unmarked car pulled up outside the house, I just didn't dare look. I heard McGurk gasp and I thought, "Oh, no! He's seen something horrible. Wanda's body in the snow. Or Willie's. Or poor little Brains standing at the window, with the man's gun at his head."

Even the squealing brakes and slamming doors behind us did nothing to cheer me. The tactical unit was probably too late.

But then I heard another noise—a more familiar, homely, scraping and swishing noise—and Lieutenant Kaspar murmuring, "I'll be darned!"—and I opened my eyes.

Bodies? Guns? Blood?

Forget it!

What I saw was those three friends of ours shoveling and sweeping like mad in the driveway. It was practically clear already, all the way down to the street. And there was Fitch at the front door—coat and hat on, bags packed.

"Looks like we're just in time," said Kaspar. "He must have suckered those friends of yours into helping him with his getaway."

McGurk's face was burning with shame.

"The dumb, stupid—"

Then he broke off. His eyes popped. And suddenly he was laughing.

We all were.

Because even before he'd seen the police cars, Fitch was fit to be tied. He was shaking one of his crutches at Willie and the others.

"*You little creeps!*" he was yelling. "*You—you—*"

He was nearly choking with rage.

And no wonder.

The snow from the driveway had been piled up neatly. But not along the edges. Oh, no!

It had been piled up neatly, efficiently, and very high, all along the front of the garage doors—making a huge barrier there. With a smaller barrier across the front porch itself. Smaller, but still too big for a man with crutches and a leg in a cast to get through in a hurry.

"Thought you'd never get here," said Brains cheerfully, tipping his cap at Lieutenant Kaspar. "This was Wanda's idea," he added modestly.

"It would never have worked without Willie's muscle," said Wanda, blushing, modest herself. "He shoveled like ten men!"

"Aw, come on!" muttered Willie.

The only one who wasn't modest was—well, guess who?

"Look at the spy now!" he jeered, pointing to Fitch, who had slumped down on his suitcases in despair. "The *snowbound* spy!" Then McGurk turned to the lieutenant, his eyes glowing. "I train my officers real good, don't you think, Leon—uh— *sir*?"

15 Loose Ends

Lieutenant Kaspar had been right. Fitch really was an ex-Government agent. Just as Bill Gonzales, the security officer at Foto-Make, Inc., was an ex-cop.

"We all have to do *something* when we retire," said Lieutenant Kaspar.

"Sure!" said Bill Gonzales. "Except some of us don't turn crooked."

We liked Mr. Gonzales. He was tall, dark, with warm brown eyes and grizzled hair. We met him in Lieutenant Kaspar's office a few days later. He was the one who tied up the few loose ends.

"The guy you called Earflaps—his real name is Dawson, by the way—worked as a clerk in our records office. He met Fitch while he was on vacation. Had a few drinks and talked about our new full-color copier. Fitch set it up then. Decided on the week when the head of Records always visits his mother in Miami. The week when Dawson would have his best chance to sneak material out of the files."

"The rat!" said McGurk.

"Yes, well, he's gonna be paying for it," said Mr. Gonzales. "But as I was about to say: what went wrong was exactly what Fitch told you. His broken leg plus the snow—coming when it did, and staying around. In the very week they'd planned."

"Sir!" said Wanda—who seemed to have a crush on Mr. Gonzales, the way she was looking at him. "Couldn't Earflaps—er—Dawson—just have *brought* the plans to the house?"

"No, honey," said the security officer. "Too risky. They didn't want to be seen together in this town, in case word got back. So Fitch decided to use his old tricks. Drops and pickups."

"And that's why he needed *us*," said Brains. "Just like he said."

"Yeah," Lieutenant Kaspar chimed in. "Except the codes were just malarky. Dawson picked the spots, knowing the town well, and phoned in with each location the day before. Fitch himself changed it into code—something to occupy your minds. Keep you from getting too snoopy. Right, Bill?"

"That's just about it, Leonard. A good idea too. Up to a point."

"Yes!" said McGurk. "The point where he got careless over the paper he used. And *I* spotted it!"

"Anyway," said Mr. Gonzales, "our new model is safe now. Thanks to you. *All* of you. . . . The only thing I need to know is this. Did you make a copy of that page? Or memorize any of it?"

His face was grave as he looked at each of us in turn.

We shook our heads.

"Nothing much," said Brains. "Only what Joey put in his notebook—about the price and the full-color bit and the model number."

"I did *think* of making a copy of it," I confessed. "Only for evidence, to bring to the lieutenant. But there wasn't time to take it to the library and use the photocopy machine there. We were late getting back to Fitch already."

"Good!" said Mr. Gonzales, smiling. "Double good, in fact! Good you didn't and good to know you could use a copying machine in your—uh—more normal investigations."

"Well, sure," I said, wondering why this should please him so much. "But those machines are expensive and—"

"Because that's just what I have here," said Mr. Gonzales, winking at the lieutenant and reaching for something behind the desk. He laid it on top. It looked like a large gray plastic box. My heart skipped a beat—and I was right! "Not the latest model," said the security officer, lifting the lid. "Just for black and white copies. But very easy to use, and portable." He stood back and waved at it with a flourish. "For you guys. A thank-you gift from the Foto-Make Organization to the McGurk Organization!"

We clustered around, gasping out our thanks and "you-shouldn't-haves."

The lieutenant and his old friend sat back and enjoyed our delight.

Then McGurk took charge.

"O.K., men. Let's get back to HQ. We can put this to use right away."

We stared at him.

"Yeah!" said McGurk, replacing the lid. "Joey—you have some new ID cards to make out. Remember? . . . Well, *this* way you need only type one—leaving blank spaces. Then we photcopy five sets and fill in the blanks separately." He scowled. "With *up-to-date* information, this time!" He turned to Kaspar, smirking. "It'll look more professional, right, Leona—Lieutenant?"

Kaspar isn't a detective for nothing. He caught *that* near-slip over his name. *He* scowled, too.

Then he relaxed, grinned, winked at Gonzales and said:

"Go on! Get outa here! All of you!"

That McGurk! He's one terrible slave-driver. Even his buddy and fellow slave-driver *Leonard* looked pityingly at me as we trooped out with our new treasure.

He must have guessed I was going to have to sweat over those ID cards for hours and hours, until McGurk decided they were really "professional-looking" at last!